the Lemonade Hurricane

A STORY OF
MINDFULNESS AND
MEDITATION

Licia Morelli

Illustrated by Jennifer E. Morris

My name is Emma.

My days are busy and full.

Sometimes I like to stop and rest.

This is Henry.

Henry likes to run, wrestle,
roar, and drink lemonade.

I call him The Lemonade Hurricane.

Henry's days are busy and full.

Sometimes too busy
and too full.

Then Henry gets wild.

When Henry gets like this I try to stay out of the way...

I really don't like hurricanes.

I wish Henry could calm down sometimes.

I wish I could show him how.

Then we could play together.

Henry's fun when he's not a hurricane.

Maybe I can show Henry
how to be still.

The next day...

"Watch this," I say.

Sit.   Bow.   Breathe.

Breathe.

"When I sit I can feel the ground beneath me.
I can hear the birds chirping.
I can smell the grass."

"When I bow I pretend I am on top of a mountain and can see for miles and miles."

"And when I breathe, I pretend I'm the wind moving the leaves in the trees."

"I can do it too," says Henry.

Henry pretends he is on top of an elephant and has to bow really slowly so he does not fall off.

Look.
Listen.
Feel.
Breathe.

I take deep breaths.
Henry takes deep breaths.
We look, listen, feel, and smell.

The Lemonade Hurricane is gone.

THICHT NAHT HANH, a Vietnamese Buddhist monk, tells a story in the book *Planting Seeds* about a young girl named Thuy who was staying at the hermitage (a remote village) where Thicht Naht Hanh was living. One day she asked Thicht Naht Hanh for something to drink, and he offered her a glass of organic apple juice.

Thuy did not want to drink the apple juice because of the pulp suspended in it, so she left the glass on a table and went outdoors to play. When she returned an hour later, she saw that the apple juice looked very clear. All of the sediment had sunk to the bottom of the glass. When she asked how that could have happened, Thicht Naht Hanh told her that the glass had been practicing sitting meditation, and by keeping still had become clear.

Lemonade is like apple juice. When it's stirred up, pulp swirls around inside the glass. When it sits quietly, things settle and the liquid becomes clear. In this way, a glass of lemonade is a metaphor for how meditation and mindfulness work. That is why this book is called *The Lemonade Hurricane*. Practicing mindfulness and meditation helps us tame the hurricane within.

Meditation cushions are used during mindfulness and meditation practice.

A *zafu* is a round or crescent-shaped cushion that you sit on. It is sometimes filled with buckwheat. A *gomden* is a firm rectangular block that does not change shape and can be used instead of a zafu. A *zabuton* is a square, flat cushion that goes underneath the zafu or gomden and provides a soft floor for knees and ankles.

While mats are often used, they are not necessary for meditating. You can also sit on a rolled-up towel, a yoga mat, or right on the floor.

Sit.

Bow.

Breathe.

How to Bow

- Sit up very straight with your legs crossed.
- Place your hands—palms together, fingers up—in front of your heart.
- Breathe in.
- Breathe out, bending slowly forward.
- Breathe in while returning to the very straight sitting position.

How to Meditate while Lying Down

- Lie on your back with a stuffed animal or soft object on your belly.
- As you breathe in and out, observe how the object rises and falls.
- Keep breathing in and out, and notice how high and low the object goes with deep breaths.
- If the object tips over or falls off your belly, quietly place it back on and begin again.
- See how long you can watch the object rising and falling.

[adapted from *Sensational Meditation for Children: Child Friendly Meditation Techniques Based on the Five Senses*, by Sarah Wood Vallely]

How to Practice Mindfulness and Meditation

- Find a place to sit—on the floor or in a chair.
- Once seated and quiet, bow.
- After bowing, place your hands on your thighs or in your lap and look down and forward, about two feet in front of you.
- Feel your breath flowing in and out (placing a finger under your nose or a hand on your belly will help you feel this).
- After you feel your breath go in and out a few times, place your hands back on your thighs.

- Start to count your breaths. Breathe in and count one; breathe out and count one. Breathe in and count two; breathe out and count two. Breathe in and count three; breathe out and count three— and keep going. Try to get to ten without daydreaming!
- You can also try focusing on something while you practice your breathing. It can be a shell, a rock, a marble—anything you want. Place the object in front of you while you are sitting, and look at it as you breathe in and out.

- Set a timer and try practicing for three minutes. Add more time as you practice more.
- When you are done, bow once more.

How did sitting feel?

Did you find yourself thinking about other things? What number did you get to without daydreaming? How many times did you have to start over?

Do you know that people have more than 48 thoughts per minute? That is almost one thought per second—70,000 thoughts per day! What kind of thoughts do you have? When you are breathing in and out, do the thoughts come faster or slower? When you know you are thinking, is it hard to start counting your breaths again?

TILBURY HOUSE PUBLISHERS

12 Starr Street
Thomaston, Maine 04861
800-582-1899
www.tilburyhouse.com

First hardcover edition: August 2015
ISBN 978-0-88448-396-0
eBook ISBN 978-0-88448-457-8

Library of Congress Cataloging-in-Publication Data

Morelli, Licia, 1978-

The lemonade hurricane : a story about mindfulness and meditation / Licia Morelli ; illustrated by Jennifer E. Morris. -- First hardcover edition.

pages cm

Summary : "Emma's little brother Henry is a good kid--but when his day has been too busy and too full, Henry can become a hurricane! Emma wishes that she could teach Henry to be still. One day, she shows Henry how meditation can make a big difference in both their lives"-- Provided by publisher.

ISBN 978-0-88448-396-0 (hardcover : alk. paper)

ISBN 978-0-88448-457-8 (ebook : alk. paper)

[1. Meditation--Fiction. 2. Brothers and sisters--Fiction.]

I. Morris, J. E. (Jennifer E.), illustrator. II. Title.

PZ7.1.M6695Le 2015

[E]--dc23

2015007749

Designed by Ann Casady

Printed in Malaysia by Times Offset (M) Sdn. Bhd. through Four Colour Print Group, Louisville, Kentucky

(June 2015) 54425-0 / TOM 235257